Hedgehogs Don't Eat Hamburgers

Vivian French

Illustrated by Chris Fisher

PUFFIN BOOKS

Published by the Penguin Group
Penguin Books Ltd, 27 Wrights Lane, London W8 5TZ, England
Penguin Books USA Inc., 375 Hudson Street, New York, New York 10014, USA
Penguin Books Australia Ltd, Ringwood, Victoria, Australia
Penguin Books Canada Ltd, 10 Alcorn Avenue, Toronto, Ontario, Canada M4V 3B2
Penguin Books (NZ) Ltd, 182–190 Wairau Road, Auckland 10, New Zealand

Penguin Books Ltd, Registered Offices: Harmondsworth, Middlesex, England

Hedgehogs Don't Eat Hamburgers first published in Puffin Books 1993
The Hedgehogs and the Big Bag first published in Puffin Books 1994
A Puffin Book exclusively for School Book Fairs 1995
1 3 5 7 9 10 8 6 4 2

Text copyright © Vivian French, 1993, 1994
Illustrations copyright © Chris Fisher, 1993, 1994
All rights reserved

The moral right of the author and illustrator has been asserted

Filmset in Monotype Bembo Schoolbook

Printed in England by Clays Ltd, St Ives plc

Contents

HEDGEHOGS DON'T EAT HAMBURGERS

Hector saw a picture on a paper bag.

"What's that?" he asked.

"That's a hamburger," said his dad.

"Can I have one for my tea?"
asked Hector.

"No," said his dad. "Hedgehogs
don't eat hamburgers."

"I do," said Hector. "And I'm
going to go and find one for my
tea."

Hector set off to find a hamburger.

"Here I go, here I go, here I go," he sang as he walked along.

Hattie popped out to see who was going by.

"Hello," said Hector. "I'm going to find my tea."

"Would you like some fine fat snails?" Hattie asked.

"No thank you," said Hector.
"I'm going to find a hamburger."

"Hedgehogs don't eat
hamburgers," said Hattie.

"I do," said Hector.

"Oh," said Hattie. "Maybe I'll
come too."

So she did.

Hector and Hattie set off to find a hamburger.

"Here we go, here we go, here we go," they sang as they walked along.

Harry popped out to see who was going by.

"Hello," said Hector. "We're
going to find my tea."

"Would you like some slow
slimy slugs?" Harry asked. "I've
got plenty."

"No thank you," said Hector.
"I'm going to find a hamburger."

"Hedgehogs don't eat
hamburgers," said Harry.

"I do," said Hector.

"Oh," said Harry. "Maybe I'll
come too."

So he did.

Hector and Hattie and Harry set off to find a hamburger.

"Here we go, here we go, here we go," they sang as they walked along.

Hester popped out to see who was going by.

"Hello," said Hector. "We're going to find my tea."

"Would you like some big black beetles?" Hester asked. "I've got lots."

"No thank you," said Hector.

"I'm going to find a hamburger."

"Hedgehogs don't eat hamburgers," said Hester.

"I do," said Hector.

"Oh," said Hester. "Maybe I'll come too."

So she did.

Hector and Hattie and Harry and Hester set off to find a hamburger.

"Here we go, here we go, here we go," they sang as they walked along.

Fox popped out to see who was going by.

"Hello," said Hector. "We're going to find my tea."

"Tea, eh?" said Fox. "What a good idea." He looked at the fat little hedgehogs, and he licked his lips.

"I'm going to find a hamburger," said Hector.

"WHAT a good idea," said Fox. "Shall I show you the way?"

"YES PLEASE," said Hector.

Hector and Hattie and Harry and
Hester set off after Fox.

"Here we go, here we go, here
we go," they sang as they walked
along.

"SSSHHH!" said Fox.

"Oh," said Hector and Hattie
and Harry and Hester.

They walked up the hill and
down the hill.

"Are we nearly there?" asked
Hector.

"Nearly," said Fox. He sniffed
the air. "Yes, we're nearly there."

Hector sniffed the air too.
"What is it?" he asked.

"That's the smell of the town,"
said Fox. "That's where the
hamburgers are."

"Oh," said Hector. He sniffed the air again. He could smell cars, and smoke, and shops, and houses. He could smell danger. "Maybe I don't want a hamburger today. Maybe I'll have big black beetles, or slow slimy slugs, or fine fat snails. Maybe hedgehogs don't eat hamburgers after all."

Hector turned round, and Hattie and Harry and Hester all turned round too.

"Here we go, here we go, here we go!" they sang.

"JUST A MINUTE," said Fox, and he opened his mouth wide. His teeth were sharp and white. "What about MY tea?"

"YOU can have a hamburger," said Hector.

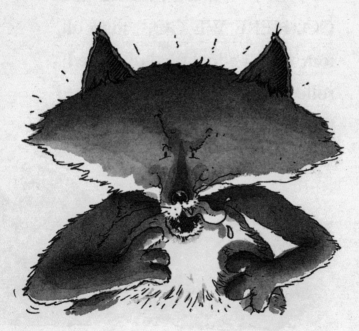

"But I don't WANT a
hamburger," said Fox. "I want
little fat HEDGEHOGS!" And he
jumped at Hector and Hattie and
Harry and Hester.

"HERE WE GO, HERE WE
GO, HERE WE GO," sang all
four little hedgehogs, and they
rolled themselves up tightly into
four prickly balls.

"OWWWW!" said Fox as he hurt his nose. "OW! OW! OW!" He turned round and ran up the hill and down the hill. He didn't stop running until he got home to his mummy.

Hector and Hattie and Harry and Hester looked at each other.

"Let's go home," said Hector.

So they all set off to go home.

"Home we go, home we go, home we go," they sang as they walked up the hill and down the hill. And they got home just in time to have fine fat snails, slow slimy slugs and big black beetles for their tea.

THE HEDGEHOGS' SONG

The sun was going down in the
sky, and the birds were singing
their last songs. Hector was
singing too.

"SSSH!" said his dad.

"What are you doing?" asked
Hector.

"Listening," said his dad.

"Oh," said Hector. "What for?"

"I'm listening for things that wriggle," said his dad.

"Things that wriggle are
sometimes big and sometimes little.
Sometimes they are dangerous, but
sometimes they are good to eat.
Wriggly white grubs are VERY
good to eat."

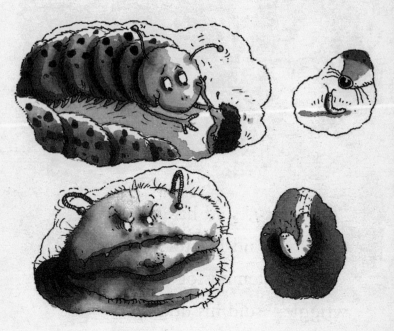

"Shall I sing you my song?" asked
Hector. "Then you can listen to
me instead. It's a song about Big
Bad Badger."

"Hush!" said his dad. "You must always be polite to Badger, or he might fancy YOU for his tea."

"Not me," said Hector. "I'm MUCH too clever."

Hector went to see Hattie. Hattie was sitting under a beech tree, where the dry leaves lay thickly on the ground.

"What are you doing?" he asked.

"Listening," said Hattie.

"Oh," said Hector. "What for?"

"I'm listening for things that rustle," said Hattie. "Things that rustle are sometimes big and sometimes little. Sometimes they are dangerous, but sometimes they are good to eat."

"Shall I sing you my song?" Hector said. "Then you can listen to me instead."

"All right," said Hattie.

Hector sang,

"Big bad badger
Looking for his tea.
Pull his tail, make him wail
One two three!"

"That's nice," said Hattie. "Let's
go and sing it to Harry."

Hector and Hattie went to see
Harry. Harry was sitting under a
bramble bush, where the
blackberries grew.

"What are you doing?" they
asked.

"Listening," said Harry.

"Oh," said Hector. "What for?"

"I'm listening for things that creep," said Harry. "Things that creep are sometimes big and sometimes little. Sometimes they are dangerous, but sometimes they are good to eat."

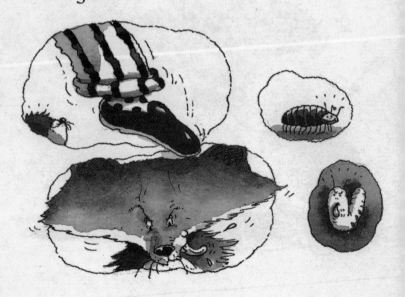

"Shall we sing you a song?" asked Hector. "Then you can listen to us instead."

"All right," said Harry.

So Hector and Hattie sang their song.

"That's nice," said Harry, when they had finished singing. "Let's go and sing it to Hester."

Hector and Hattie and Harry
went to see Hester. Hester was
standing near an old stone wall.

"What are you doing?" they
asked.

"Listening," said Hester.

"Oh," said Hector. "What for?"

"I'm listening for things that slither," said Hester. "Things that slither are sometimes big and sometimes little. Sometimes they are dangerous, but sometimes they are good to eat."

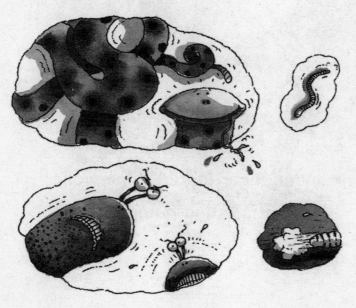

"Shall we sing you a song?" asked Hector. "Then you can listen to us instead."

"All right," said Hester.

So Hector and Hattie and Harry sang their song.

"That's nice," said Hester. "Let's
go and sing it while we walk
through the woods."

Hector and Hattie and Harry and
Hester sang as they walked
through the woods.

"Big bad badger
Looking for his tea.
Pull his tail, make him wail
One two three!"

They walked under the beech
trees, where the dry leaves lay
thick on the ground. Big things
and little things rustled in the
leaves, but Hector and Hattie and
Harry and Hester didn't hear
them.

They walked under the bramble bushes, where the blackberries grew. Big things and little things were creeping all around, but Hector and Hattie and Harry and Hester didn't hear them.

They walked along beside
the old stone wall.

Big things and little things
slithered up and down it, but
Hector and Hattie and Harry and
Hester didn't hear them.

"Let's sing our song to the
birds," said Hector.

They climbed right up to the top
of the wall and began to sing.

"Big bad badger," sang Hector
and Hattie and Harry and Hester.

Hester heard a noise, and
looked down. "Oh!" she said, and

stopped singing.

"Looking for his tea," sang
Hector and Hattie and Harry.

Hattie heard a noise, and
looked down. "Oh!" she said, and
stopped singing.

"Pull his tail, make him wail,"
sang Hector and Harry.

Harry heard a noise and looked
down. "Oh!" he said, and stopped
singing.
"ONE TWO THREE!" sang
Hector, at the top of his voice.

"WHAT a noisy little
hedgehog!" said a very loud voice
from the bottom of the wall.

"OH!" said Hector. "OH!…
Hello, Mr Badger."

Badger looked up at Hector and
Hattie and Harry and Hester.

"I'm very fond of a song," he
said. "Sing your song to me."

"If you say so, Mr Badger,"
said Hector.

"I do," said Badger. "And hurry
up about it."

Hector began to sing.

"Big brave badger

Looking for his tea.

Caught a snail, made it wail

One two three!"

"I see," said Badger. "And are you sure that it wasn't a silly little hedgehog that was caught?"

Hector shook his head. "Not this time, Mr Badger," he said. "And next time I'll be looking out."

"Next time," said Badger, "you might not be on the top of a wall." And he turned and trotted away.

"Phew!" said Hector.

"I want to go home," said Hattie.

"Me too," said Harry.

"And me," said Hester.

"Shall we sing my song?" Hector
asked.

"NO!" said Hattie and Harry
and Hester.

They went home very quietly.
They climbed back down the wall
and they heard big and little
things slithering beside them.

They crept under the bramble
bushes and they heard big things
and little things creeping all
around them.

They tiptoed under the beech
trees and they heard big things
and little things rustling with them
through the dry leaves.

Hector's dad was waiting for him. "You can sing your song to me now," he said. "I've caught plenty of wriggly white grubs for our dinner."

"All right," said Hector.

He sang,

> "Clever little hedgehogs
> Looking all around.
> Tiptoe here and tiptoe there
> Never make a sound!"

Hector went indoors to eat
wriggly white grubs, and Hattie
and Harry and Hester tiptoed all
the way home.

The Hedgehogs and
the Big Bag

Vivian French

Illustrated by Chris Fisher

Hector was getting ready to go
out.

"Where are you going?" asked
his dad.

"I'm going to go to the very
middle of the woods," said Hector.
"I'm going to catch my dinner."

"Well," said his dad, "be
careful."

Hector went round to see Hattie.

"I'm going to go to the very middle of the woods," he said. "I'm going to catch my dinner. Will you come too?"

"All right," said Hattie. "Let's catch some grasshoppers."

Hector and Hattie went to see
Harry.

"We're going to go to the very
middle of the woods," said Hector.
"We're going to catch our dinner.
Will you come too?"

"All right," said Harry. "Let's
catch some snails."

Hector and Hattie and Harry
went to see Hester.

"We're going to go to the very
middle of the woods," said Hector.
"We're going to catch our dinner.
Will you come too?"

"All right," said Hester. "Let's
catch some wriggly worms."

Hector, Hattie, Harry and Hester
ran through the long grass.

"Are we nearly there?" asked
Hattie. "I'm getting hungry."

"It's not far now," said Hector.

"Good," said Hattie.

Hector, Hattie, Harry and Hester
walked underneath the bracken.

"Are we nearly there? asked
Harry. "I'm getting hungry."

"It's not far now," said Hector.

"Good," said Harry.

Hector, Hattie, Harry and Hester
crept under the brambles.

"I'm getting VERY hungry,"
said Hester. "Are we nearly
there?"

"It's not far now," said Hector.

"Good," said Hester.

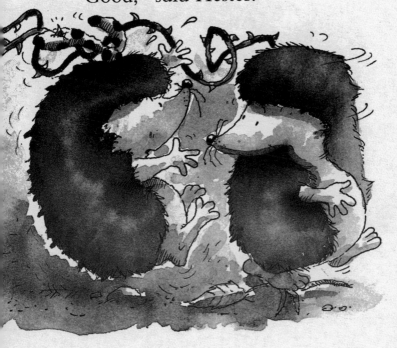

Hector, Hattie, Harry and Hester
reached the very middle of the
woods.

"Oh!" said Hector.

"Where are the grasshoppers?"
asked Hattie.

"Where are the snails?" asked
Harry.

"Where are the wriggly worms?"
asked Hester. "I'm VERY hungry."

Hector scratched his nose.
"Perhaps we should go home
again," he said.

"NO!" said Hattie and Harry
and Hester. "We want to have a
rest!"

"All right," said Hector, and
they all sat down.

Hector and Hattie and Harry and
Hester closed their eyes.

Hector and Hattie and Harry and
Hester went to sleep.

At the other end of the wood, Fox was getting ready to go out. He went to find his big bag.

"Where are you going?" asked his mum.

"I'm going to go to the very middle of the woods," said Fox. "I'm going to catch my dinner."

"Well," said his mum, "be careful."

Fox caught three grasshoppers and put them in his big bag. Then he went skipping over the grass.

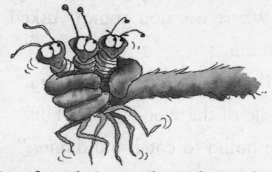

Fox found six snails and put them in his big bag. Then he went jumping over the bracken.

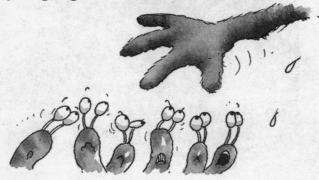

Fox snapped up eight wriggly
worms and popped them in his big
bag. Then he went hopping over
the brambles.

Fox reached the very middle of the woods.

"Well, well, well," he said. "What have we got here?" He looked at Hector and Hattie and Harry and Hester, and he tiptoed right up to them.

"BOO!" shouted Fox.

Hector and Hattie and Harry and
Hester woke up with a jump.

"Hee hee!" laughed Fox. "This
is better than grasshoppers or snails
or wriggly worms. Now, which of
you shall I put in my big bag?"

Hector and Hattie and Harry and
Hester looked at each other.
Hector winked at Hattie, and
Hattie winked at Harry. Harry
winked at Hester, and Hester
winked at Hector. Then they
looked at Fox.

"I'm fat," said Hector.

"But I'm fatter," said Hattie.

"I'm tasty," said Harry.

"But I'm tastier," said Hester.

They all held hands and danced in
a circle round and round Fox.

"All of us are rather fat,
None of us are thinner,
Hurry, hurry, Mr Fox
Come and choose your dinner!"

"Stop it!" said Fox. "You're
making me giddy."

Hector and Hattie and Harry and Hester went faster and faster and faster.

"Thinner, fatter,
Fatter, thinner,
Which of us
Is Foxy's dinner?"

Fox spun round and round in the
middle.

"Stop it!" he snapped. "Stop it!"

Hector and Hattie and Harry and
Hester went on spinning.

"Dinner, dinner, dinner, dinner.
Ready, steady, go!" said Hector.

They each spun away into the
brambles and curled up into neat
little balls.

"Oops, I feel giddy!" said Fox,
and he fell over in a heap.

"Ouch!" he said, and sat up. He rubbed his eyes and looked all around.

"No dinner," he said. "Nothing to put in my big bag." He rubbed his eyes again, and began to sniff and snuffle.

Hector heard Fox sniffing.

"Cunning little Fox," he said to himself. "He's trying his foxy tricks." And he stayed just where he was.

Hattie heard Fox sniffing.

"Cunning little Fox," she said to herself. "He's trying his foxy tricks."

And she stayed just where she was.

Harry heard Fox snuffling.

"Cunning little Fox," he said to himself. "He's trying his foxy tricks."

And he stayed just where he was.

Hester heard Fox snuffling.

"Poor little Fox," she said to herself. "He sounds so sad." She uncurled herself and ran over to see him.

"Don't cry, Fox," Hester said.

"I WON'T!" said Fox, and there wasn't a sign of a sniffle or a snuffle. With a bounce and a bound he pushed Hester over. With one pat of his paw he rolled her into his big bag.

"Grasshoppers, snails, wriggly worms and a fat little hedgehog!" said Fox. "What a wonderful, wonderful dinner I've caught!"

And he began to walk home,
dragging his big bag behind him.

Hector and Hattie and Harry
came hurrying out from under the
brambles.

"Quick!" said Hector, and they
scurried after Fox.

"Mr Fox! Mr Fox!
Wait for us!" shouted
Hector.

Fox looked behind him. "What is it?"

"You haven't caught me!" Hector said. "I want to be caught as well!"

"And me!" said Hattie.

"And me!" said Harry.

Fox stopped and scratched his
head. "Are you sure?" he asked.

"Oh, YES!" said Hector and
Hattie and Harry.

"I don't think it's quite usual,"
Fox said. "I think you ought to
run away."

"Oh, NO!" said Hector and
Hattie and Harry.

Fox sat down to think. Hester
poked her nose out of the big bag.

"Why have we stopped?" she
asked.

"We want to come too,"
Hector explained. "But Fox
doesn't think we should."

Fox shook his head. "I don't
know what to think," he said.

"There's plenty of room in the
bag," Hester said. "It's a very BIG
bag."

Hector looked at Fox. "Will your
mummy be pleased if you catch
one fat little hedgehog?" he asked.

Fox nodded.

"Then," said Hector, "she'll be
VERY, VERY pleased if you catch
four fat little hedgehogs."

Fox looked more cheerful.

"Yes," he said.

Hector patted Fox's head. "That's all right then." And he opened up the big bag and walked in.

"Thank you very much, Fox," said Hattie, and she walked in too.

"Thank you very much, Fox,"
said Harry. He walked in after
Hattie and closed the bag behind
him.

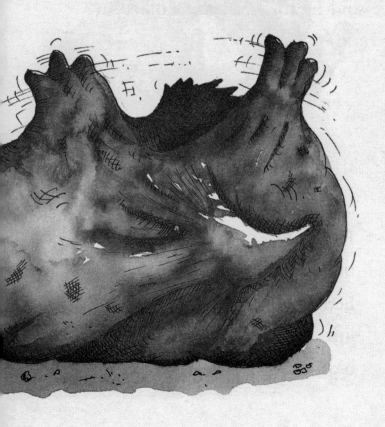

Fox got slowly to his feet. He
thought about the four fat little
hedgehogs, and he licked his
lips. Then he took hold of the
big bag . . .

"OH!" said Fox.

"What's the matter?" asked Hector, popping his head out.

"It's too heavy," Fox said.

"Shall we eat the grasshoppers and the snails and the wriggly worms?" Hector asked. "That would make the bag lighter."

"All right," said Fox.

"We won't be long," said Hector, and he popped in again.

Fox sat down and waited.

"We've finished!" Hector called.
"Try again!"

Fox got up and took hold of the
big bag . . .

"Bother!" said Fox.

"What's the matter?" asked
Hattie, popping her head out.

"It's still too heavy," said Fox.

"Ah," said Hattie, "you'll have
to try harder." And she popped
back into the big bag.

Fox pulled.

And he heaved.

And he heaved.

And he pulled.

He puffed.

    And he panted.

    And he panted.

    And he puffed.

And he heaved.

And he pulled.

And he heaved once more . . .

"It's no good," puffed Fox, and he
flopped on the ground. "The big
bag is too heavy."

Hector popped out again. "My word, Fox," he said. "You do look tired."

"I am," said Fox.

"Shall we take turns?" Hector asked. "You pull us, and then we'll pull you?"

"All right," said Fox. "And it's
your turn now."

Hector and Hattie and Harry and
Hester walked out of the big bag.

"Here you are," said Hector,
and he held it open.

"Thank you very much," said
Fox, and he walked inside.

Hector winked at Hattie, and
Hattie winked at Harry. Harry
winked at Hester, and Hester
winked at Hector.

"Are you quite comfortable,
Fox?" Hector called.

"Yes, thank you," Fox called
back.

Hector and Hattie and Harry and
Hester took tight hold of the big
bag. They tied up the top one
way, and they tied it up another
way. They tied it up with four big
knots. Then they pulled and they
heaved, and they heaved and they
pulled the big bag until it was
outside Fox's own front door.

"Goodbye, Fox!" they called. "We hope you have a lovely dinner!"

Hector, Hattie, Harry and Hester
ran all the way home.

"Would you like some dinner?"
asked Hector's dad.

"No, thank you," said Hector.
"We've had it."

"We had grasshoppers," said
Hattie.

"And snails," said Harry.

"And wriggly worms," said Hester.

"Goodness me!" said Hector's dad.
"What a lot of things you caught
in the middle of the woods!"

"Yes," said Hector, "we're very
good at catching things!"

And Hector and Hattie and Harry
and Hester all laughed and
laughed and laughed.

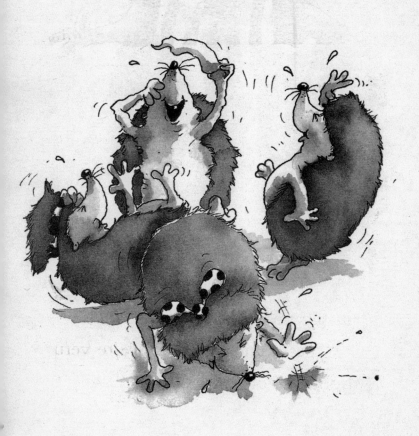